Saxton Freymann **TOMIE DEPAOLA**

Dan Yaccarino **PETER H. REYNOLDS**

SOPHIE BLACKALL Yumi Heo

Boris Kulikov BRETT HELQUIST

HENRY COLE Judy Schachner

Chris Raschka LAURIE KELLER

DAVID SMALL Jon J Muth

KNOCK, KNOCK!

DIAL BOOKS
FOR YOUNG READERS

DIAL BOOKS FOR YOUNG READERS

A division of Penguin Young Readers Group

Published by The Penguin Group • Penguin Group (USA) Inc., 375 Hudson Street,
New York, NY 10014, U.S.A. • Penguin Group (Canada), 90 Eglinton Avenue East, Suite 700,
Toronto, Ontario, Canada M4P 2Y3 (a division of Pearson Penguin Canada Inc.) •
Penguin Books Ltd, 80 Strand, London WC2R 0RL, England • Penguin Ireland, 25 St. Stephen's
Green, Dublin 2, Ireland (a division of Penguin Books Ltd) • Penguin Group (Australia),
250 Camberwell Road, Camberwell, Victoria 3124, Australia (a division of Pearson Australia Group Pty Ltd) •
Penguin Books India Pvt Ltd, 11 Community Centre, Panchsheel Park, New Delhi - 110 017, India •
Penguin Group (NZ), Cnr Airborne and Rosedale Roads, Albany, Auckland 1310,
New Zealand (a division of Pearson New Zealand Ltd) • Penguin Books (South Africa) (Pty) Ltd, 24 Sturdee
Avenue, Rosebank, Johannesburg 2196, South Africa • Penguin Books Ltd, Registered Offices: 80 Strand,
London WC2R 0RL, England • Pages 15–16 copyright © 2007 by Sophie Blackall; pages 23–24 copyright © 2007
by Henry Cole; pages 9–10 copyright © 2007 by Tomie dePaola; pages 7–8 copyright © 2007 by Play With Your Food LLC;
pages 21–22 copyright © 2007 by Brett Helquist; pages 17–18 copyright © 2007 by Yumi Heo;
pages 29–30 copyright © 2007 by Laurie Keller; pages 19–20 copyright © 2007 by Boris Kulikov;
pages 33–34 copyright © 2007 by Jon J. Muth; pages 27–28 copyright © 2007 by Chris Raschka;
pages 13–14 copyright © 2007 by Peter H. Reynolds; pages 25–26 copyright © 2007 by Judith Byron Schachner;
pages 31–32 copyright © 2007 by David Small; pages 11–12 copyright © 2007 by Dan Yaccarino •
The illustrations on pages 36–37 are the copyrighted property of the respective illustrator.

Designed by Teresa Dikun • Manufactured in China on acid-free paper

1 3 5 7 9 10 8 6 4 2

Library of Congress Cataloging-in-Publication Data

Knock, knock! / Saxton Freymann . . . [et al.].

p. cm. ISBN-13: 978-0-8037-3152-3

1. Knock-knock jokes. 2. Wit and humor, Juvenile. I. Freymann, Saxton.

PN6231.K55K56 2007   818'.60208—dc22

2006039463

KNOCK, KNOCK!

Who's there?
Lettuce.
Lettuce **who**?

KNOCK, KNOCK!
WHO'S THERE?
LIONEL.
LIONEL WHO?

LION-EL EAT ME IF YOU DON'T OPEN UP THAT DOOR!

art by PETER H. REYNOLDS

Knock, knock! Who's there?

Henrietta. Henrietta who?

Henry etta whole cake!

art by **SOPHIE BLACKALL**

Knock, knock!

WHO'S THERE?

Ice cream.

Ice cream WHO?

I scream, **YOU** scream, we **all** scream for **ice cream.**

art by YUMI HE

art by BORIS KULIKOV

Knock, knock! Who's THERE?
Ima. Ima who?

art by HENRY COLE

"Wildebeest be dining alone tonight?"

art by JUDY SCHACHNER

art by **CHRIS RASCHKA**

Knock,
knock!

Come in!

art by JON J MUTH

knock, knock!

who's
there?

TURN the PAGE
and FIND OUT!

WHO DO THESE ARTISTS WANT

JON J MUTH

> I wish it were my younger self, then I'd tell him to be good!

Jon J Muth's books include: *Zen Shorts, The Three Questions,* and *Stone Soup*

SOPHIE BLACKALL

> Anyone bearing cake.

Sophie Blackall's books include: *Meet Wild Boars* by Meg Rosoff, *Ruby's Wish* by Shirin Yim, and *Ivy and Bean* by Annie Barrows

> Sam and Janet! Sam and Janet WHO?
>
> "SAM AN' JANET EVENING."

TOMIE DEPAOLA

Tomie dePaola's books include: *26 Fairmount Avenue, Christmas Remembered,* and *Strega Nona*

Juan Fishtwofishredfishbluefish.

CHRIS RASCHKA

Chris Raschka's books include: *The Hello, Goodbye Window* by Norton Juster, *Five for a Little One,* and *Yo! Yes?*

SAXTON FREYMANN

> Albus Dumbledore. Or perhaps he would "turnip" as Albus PLUM-bledore. I like visitors who are loving and wise.

Saxton Freymann's books include: *Food Play, Food for Thought,* and *How Are You Peeling?*

BRETT HELQUIST

> Anybody but Ima.

Brett Helquist's books include: *Roger the Jolly Pirate, A Series of Unfortunate Events* by Lemony Snicket, and *Milly and the Macy's Parade* by Shana Corey

HENRY COLE

> Lily Tomlin with a chocolate cake, Bette Midler with a bottle of milk, & Dolly Parton with her guitar.

Henry Cole's books include: *Naughty Little Monkeys* by Jim Aylesworth, *Tubby the Tuba* by Paul Tripp, and *And Tango Makes Three* by Peter Parnell and Justin Richards

KNOCKING AT THEIR DOORS?

BORIS KULIKOV

ABBY. ABBY WHO? A big, pleasant surprise.

Boris Kulikov's books include: *Betty Lou Blue* by Nancy Crocker, *Carnival of the Animals* by John Lithgow, and *Max's Words* by Kate Banks

LAURIE KELLER

Laurie Keller's books include: *Arnie the Doughnut, The Scrambled States of America,* and *Grandpa Gazillion's Number Yard*

SpongeBob SquarePants delivering me a gigantic box of Krispy Kreme doughnuts!

DAVID SMALL

No one, unless they've called ahead first.

David Small's books include: *Once Upon a Banana* by Jennifer Armstrong, *My Senator and Me* by Senator Edward M. Kennedy, and *The Friend* by Sarah Stewart

I would like **Pink Cotton Candy** to knock on my door.

YUMI HEO

Yumi Heo's books include: *Uncle Peter's Amazing Chinese Wedding* by Lenore Look, *Tangerines and Tea* by Ona Gritz, and *Hey Mr. Choo-Choo, Where Are You Going?* by Susan Wickberg

JUDY SCHACHNER

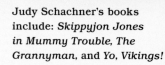

Everybody in this BOOK!

Judy Schachner's books include: *Skippyjon Jones in Mummy Trouble, The Grannyman,* and *Yo, Vikings!*

PETER H. REYNOLDS

My Fairy Godmother. I'd ask her for three wishes: for the earth to heal, world peace, and happy, and ...lthy people.

... Reynolds's books include: *The Dot, Ish,* ... Judy Moody series by Megan McDonald

I'd like to have children at my door wanting to hear a **good** story!

Dan Yaccarino's books include: *Unlovable, Zoom! Zoom! Zoom! I'm Off to the Moon!* and *Trashy Town*

DAN YACCARINO